# The Roundhouse Cat

BY FREEMAN H. HUBBARD

# THE ROUNDHOUSE CAT

## and Other Railroad Animals

WHITTLESEY HOUSE

McGraw-Hill Book Company, Inc.

New York · London · Toronto

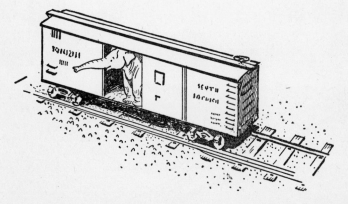

ILLUSTRATED BY KURT WIESE

# THE ROUNDHOUSE CAT
## AND OTHER RAILROAD ANIMALS

OTHER BOOKS BY FREEMAN H. HUBBARD
*Railroad Avenue*
*Vinnie Ream and Mr. Lincoln*

The story, "The Roundhouse Cat," appeared in *Story Parade* magazine. An adaptation of "Horse Sense" appeared in *The Catholic Boy*. "The Bear in the Baggage Car," "The Dining-car Goat," "The Beavers that Flooded the Tracks," and "The Circus-train Elephant" appeared in *Children's Play Mate*.

SECOND PRINTING

Published by Whittlesey House
A division of the McGraw-Hill Book Company, Inc.
Printed in the United States of America

# Contents

The Roundhouse Cat, 7

The Dining-car Goat, 23

Two Dogs on One Ticket, 40

Horse Sense, 60

The Bear in the Baggage Car, 79

The Beavers that Flooded the Track, 91

The Circus-train Elephant, 108

# The Roundhouse Cat

Tom was no ordinary black cat. He hadn't a white hair on his whole body. He never saw a kitchen, never climbed a back-yard fence, never slept in a barn, and never poked his whiskers into a garbage can. Tom was a railroad cat. He was born in the roundhouse where the engines are kept.

All day and all night his ears were filled with the rumble and roar and clank of trains, the dingdong of engine bells, and the shrill blasts of engine whistles. He loved smoke and steam and coal dust. These sounds and smells were part of his life.

Often he sat in the freight house nearby and made believe he was dozing. Secretly, though, he was watching the men as they loaded one boxcar after another with crates of fancy red apples, milk cans, or maybe boxes of fish.

These products drifted down the conveyer belt from the old freight shed into the cars that stood on the sidetrack waiting to be filled. Tom never tired of looking at it with his slanted yellow eyes.

In common with all healthy cats Tom was fond of mischief. One afternoon, just for fun, he mounted the conveyer belt and rode it down into a car. He purred with delight. This was his first ride. It pleased him so much that he quickly went back to the loading platform for another trip. He did this again and again.

After that, when Tom wanted to have fun, he amused himself on the freight conveyer. The men employed there grinned at his antics. Others came from all over Junction Town to see the sport. One fellow brought a camera and snapped a picture of Tom taking a ride. This picture was printed in the *Junction Town Daily News*. The men were proud and happy to see it.

From that day on Tom owned the freight house. Whatever he did was all right with the men. Tom knew it, too. Sometimes he purposely lay down on the busiest spot of the loading platform, but instead of shoving him aside the men let him stay. They moved themselves out of the way.

"Watch it, Tom!" they would call, or, "Here we come, Tom!"

Tom found the smell of fish exciting. When sea food was being loaded, he meowed and rubbed against the railroad men's legs. Once in a while he was lucky. A man would toss him a fish from a broken box. Tom would seize it in his jaws and vanish behind the freight shed. This was the last that would be seen of him for the day, but early the next morning he would show up again as usual.

One hot July afternoon Tom sprawled out lazily in the shade of the loading platform. The men sweated over their work. Tom felt at peace with the world. He was too drowsy to heed a blue jay that scolded him from a dying spruce tree beside the freight house. But when a chipmunk made a flying leap down that same tree—a swift streak of brown and black—Tom sprang into action.

The chipmunk landed on the conveyer belt and rode into a boxcar. Quick as a flash Tom followed. Things happened so fast that none of

the men noticed either the cat or the chipmunk. Someone shut the car door and sealed it with a metal tag. Tom was locked inside!

A switching engine backed into the car and pulled it across the railroad yard to a freight train that was almost ready to leave. Tom gazed around in the dusty darkness. He saw only boxes and barrels. These were packed so close together that he had little room to crawl between them.

He hated to be locked up. It made him angry to be bumped and jolted when the car was coupled onto the train and the train began moving.

He uttered a loud wail. It was drowned out by the hum of rolling wheels and the clank of couplers. For a whole hour he yowled and yowled, but nobody heard him. At length he curled up on a barreltop. There he fell asleep to the lullaby of wheels clicking over rail joints.

For a day and two nights Tom stayed in that car as it rolled on and on and on. Once in a while it stood still on a sidetrack. Tom meowed again and again. Nothing happened. Tom felt outraged. All he could do was glare at the inside of the dusty old boxcar.

Mr. Chipmunk kept safely out of reach. Tom often heard him pattering and scratching around the car. He hardly ever saw the small brown and black animal, and the passageways were too narrow for the twelve-pound cat to follow. Even so, there was one advantage in having Mr. Chipmunk as a fellow passenger. Tom was not alone. He enjoyed matching wits with the cunning little beast, always hoping to catch him off guard. That helped him to forget he was hungry.

Meanwhile the train rumbled across the broad

prairie. It chugged up into the foothills. It climbed the mountains. It clattered over bridges, through black tunnels and snowsheds, and finally stopped at a station.

Tom, who had seen none of this landscape, was quite discouraged. When the train halted, he heard voices outside his car and gave forth a piteous wail. Then he clawed at the door. He was tired of being locked up in the darkness. So he kept meowing and scratching until help came.

An engineer named Mr. Rayburn was passing the car on the way to his engine cab, when he heard the unhappy cat. He paused and called, "Here, kitty, kitty!"

Tom wailed louder than ever.

"Just a minute!" called the engineer. "I will get you out."

Pretty soon the door slid open, letting in a shaft of sunlight and a rush of clean mountain air. At the same time the chipmunk leaped out and scampered away. Tom blinked and sniffed. Then he left the hateful old car, sliding down the side of a barrel into Mr. Rayburn's arms.

The engineer stroked his thick black fur. Tom

purred and poked at the man's face with a vel-
vety paw as if to say, "Thank you." Mr. Rayburn
found a metal tag attached to a collar on Tom's
neck. He read the words engraved on it.

### TOM
*Western Central R.R.*

"So your name's Tom and you're a railroad
cat? Well, the Western Central is a big road, but
some day we will learn where you came from."

Tom licked the man's hand with a rough
tongue.

"I guess you're hungry." The engineer opened his lunch pail, took out a sardine and tomato sandwich, and set it on the ground. Then he got Tom a pan of water from the station.

"Who locked you up, anyhow?" he said when he returned. "Were they trying to get rid of you? Well, you're coming along with me now, if you don't mind riding in an engine cab."

When the cat finished his meal, Mr. Rayburn strode toward the engine, whistling for the cat to follow, and Tom trailed after him. He had never before ridden in an engine cab. But he had seen plenty of them and heard them and smelled their smoke and grease. So he was wise in railroad matters. Soon he felt very much at home on the engineer's seat box. It thrilled him to look out the window as the scenery flashed by.

There were snow-capped mountain peaks, silvery winding rivers, tiny stations, and a few scattered towns. Wild flowers bloomed beside the track. Tom had come from Junction Town, which lay in flat country. He found mountain life new and exciting. He was happy.

Not even the harsh clang of the fire door annoyed him when the fireman closed it after shoveling coal into the red-hot firebox. Tom gazed about with lively curiosity. His purring was lost in the deep throb of the engine's driving wheels. On, on they went.

At length, as they thundered across a wooden trestle, Mr. Rayburn said to the cat, "We're almost home now. This is Big Muddy Creek. Three miles more and we reach Coalburg."

Coalburg, at the end of his run, was a railroad town in a valley. When they reached the station, Tom sprang out of the cab. He was hungry. He sniffed his way across the station platform to the lunchroom. The smell of food was most inviting. Tom stood outside the door and meowed.

Mr. Rayburn heard the meow. He went into the lunchroom and the cat followed. Then he bought two plates of beef stew. The man-size one was for himself. And a half-size one he set down on the floor for Tom. After the meal, the cat cleaned his face with his paws and purred his thanks. But he refused to go home with Mr. Rayburn. Instead, he strolled over to the Coalburg roundhouse and spent the night there. He had been born in a roundhouse and he felt very much at home there.

At noon the next day, when Mr. Rayburn reported for duty, he was surprised to find the cat in his cab.

"Hello, Tom!" he greeted. "So you want another ride, eh? All set to go?"

The cat gave a glad meow. Mr. Rayburn patted his head. For the next three weeks, on one trip after another, Tom rode in Mr. Rayburn's engine cab. Each night he slept in the Coalburg roundhouse. Soon everyone knew him as Mr. Rayburn's Roundhouse Cat. The weather was hot and dry, the sky cloudless. Tom had the time of his life. The engineer always took enough lunch along for them both and always bought supper for Tom in the lunchroom.

Then came rain. For three days a heavy storm lashed the mountains. It made the rails slippery. It spotted the track with shimmering pools and flooded the creeks to the danger point. Big Muddy Creek, just outside of Coalburg, became a wild foaming river. Most cats like to stay home in such weather, but not Tom. He rode with Mr. Rayburn, as usual.

The storm ended on the third night. Thick white fog hid Mr. Rayburn's black engine. It seemed to smother the great electric headlight. The engineer could not see more than a few yards ahead. He was not quite sure where he was, but he knew they would soon come to the bridge over Big Muddy Creek. He planned to run very slowly over that bridge, because the creek was badly flooded.

The huge engine drove ahead in the foggy darkness, rocking a bit from side to side. Tom was hunched on the seat box just behind the engineer. Suddenly he let out a long piercing wail. Mr. Rayburn glanced around to see if the cat was hurt in any way. Tom was not hurt, but he kept on yowling. His eyes were twin balls of fire.

"Cut it out!" ordered the engineer. "There's nothing the matter with you."

"That cat is spoiled," said the fireman. "He gets too much attention."

In reply Tom snarled like a wildcat and clawed at the engineer's sleeve. Mr. Rayburn was startled. He and the fireman tried to quiet the frantic beast, but in vain.

"There's something queer about this," Mr. Rayburn said. "Tom never acted this way before. I'm going to see what's up."

He shut off steam and set the brakes. The train skidded to a stop and Mr. Rayburn swung down from the cab. When he reached the ground, he uttered a cry. The fireman piled off after him.

Neither spoke. The two men were standing on the bank of Big Muddy Creek. They gazed with pale faces and thumping hearts as Mr. Rayburn pointed. There was no bridge! The flood had washed it away!

After a while the conductor and brakeman came up in the murky darkness to see what was wrong. Mr. Rayburn was trembling.

"Fellows," he said hoarsely, "the cat saved our lives!"

The conductor gasped. "What do you mean?"

"I mean," said Mr. Rayburn in a tight voice, "that Tom started howling just before we reached this spot. If he hadn't acted so crazy—well, I would never have stopped in time and we might all have been drowned."

"He knew the bridge was down?"

"Maybe he did. I don't know. Cats have a very sharp sense of hearing. Maybe he could tell from an odd change in the sound of our wheels rolling over the rails that the track was broken off at the river bank."

Thus the roundhouse cat became a hero. His old friends back home in Junction Town, who had wondered what became of Tom, read about him in the *Daily News*. The newspaper mentioned the name tag on his collar. It was a great day at the roundhouse and the freight house. The men wrote a telegram to Mr. Rayburn and they all signed it. They all wanted Tom to come back to Junction Town.

Pretty soon Tom was on his way. The freight conveyer belt was waiting for him, and the old freight house was trimmed with flags and streamers. He had as many sardines as he could eat. Nothing was too good for the cat that had saved a train.

# The Dining-car Goat

Just as the train puffed into Basalt town, at four by the station clock, William trotted up to the depot with a small red wagon jingling at his heels. Serena Beck sat in the wagon, holding the reins stiffly and looking straight ahead.

"Whoa, William!" she called as they came to the platform.

Passengers stuck their heads out of the train windows. They grinned at the serious little girl with red pigtails. But most of all they grinned at the little goat. William had a long beard and broad horns that curled backward, and around his neck he wore a ribbon of Scotch plaid. He was a pet at the Beck ranch in Roaring Fork Valley, a short distance from the station. Almost every day Serena drove him into town to meet the Colorado Midland's afternoon train.

Long before the train could be seen from the ranch house, three short blasts of the engine whistle would echo down the valley. This signal meant the train was coming, and coming fast.

William always understood. William was smart. He knew that when the engine whistle blew three times, he had just enough time to get down to the depot for the four o'clock train.

Now, on the station platform, he sniffed eagerly as he fixed his yellow eyes on a dining car in the middle of the train. Then he began to gallop. The wagon rattled and swayed and bounced. Serena held on tightly with one hand, gripping the reins with the other.

"Whoa!" she yelled. "Whoa, William!"

"Maa-a-a," said William. "Maa-a-a." But he kept on running.

People who stood on the station platform moved out of his path. They moved quickly—all except one young man, dressed in a light gray suit and a stiff straw hat. The man had a cane and he decided to have some fun with William. Reaching out his cane, he caught the little goat by a horn and tried to hold him still for a few seconds.

William's eyes flashed. He was not hurt but he

was angry. He backed so suddenly that Serena almost fell out of her seat. Then he lowered his head and charged. The man tried to run, but William's broad horns hit the seat of his pants with a thud, and down he went. The light gray suit was mussed. The cane was broken in two. The stiff straw hat went spinning across the station platform. People standing nearby burst into laughter.

The man scrambled up the steps of the nearest railroad car. He dashed inside and slammed the door. The passengers who had been watching

from the windows were shaking with laughter. So was the conductor.

Outside, Serena was calling frantically, "Whoa, William! Whoa, William!" But the small red wagon rolled on. William was in a hurry. He knew from experience that the train never stayed in Basalt more than five minutes, and William had a dinner date. The cook on the train was expecting him.

The cook, dressed in white, with cap and apron, stood at his usual place on the station platform beside the dining car. With both hands he held a large cardboard box that William knew was full of choice table scraps. Serena got out of the wagon and waited.

"Maa-a-a," said William.

The cook smiled and set down the box. "Dinner is served," he said.

William went to work. In no time at all he gulped up the food, even the cardboard box, and looked around for more.

Just then the conductor sang out, "Aa-all abo-oard!"

People rushed for the cars. The man in a blue suit with brass buttons lifted his right arm to signal the engineer. The engine whistle gave two long wails. *Waa-a-oow! Waa-a-oow!* "Here we go!"

The wheels started to move. Faster and faster. *Chug-chug! Chug-chug!* Serena's blue eyes followed the long gleaming train until it disappeared in the hills. Then she turned to look at William. The goat was nibbling the man's stiff straw hat.

"Here, give me that hat! You mustn't eat such things!"

She put the battered straw on William's head.

It did not fit. So she tilted it against his horns and tied it there with the Scotch-plaid ribbon from his neck.

"That's to keep the sun out of your eyes," said the girl. She studied it a moment and then sat down in the wagon. "Let's go home now!"

Serena flipped the reins. William could see nothing more to eat, so he jogged up the white dusty road toward the ranch house. At the creek he stopped for a drink of water.

Serena spoke to him. "William," she said, "you do like to meet the train, don't you? I do too. Tomorrow I am going to visit Aunt Clara at Glenwood Springs. I'll be gone a day and a night but when I get back, we can meet the train again."

Early next morning Serena woke up when the summer air was still cool with mountain dew. She dressed hurriedly and packed her bag. Then she went down to the orchard to say a quick good-by to William, who was tied to an apple tree. And then she hurried back to the house where her mother was waiting in the carriage. As they drove past the orchard, Serena turned and waved to William.

"Good-by, William!" she called. "Remember what I told you!"

"Maa-a-a," said William, trying to break his rope. He did not like to be left behind.

After Serena had gone, William began to feel lonely. The day passed very slowly. Bees buzzed around the apple trees. Crickets chirped. The sun grew hotter and hotter. By and by William lay down in the shade and fell asleep.

Late that afternoon the engine whistle woke him up. The four o'clock train was steaming into Basalt. Gray clouds darkened the sky. A cool breeze swept over the valley.

William sprang to his feet and tugged at the rope. It would not break. Again and again he tugged. It was no use. The train would soon reach the station, and the cook would be waiting for him with good things to eat, but William was still tied up in the orchard.

William was frantic. Then the thought of food gave him an idea. He chewed and chewed the rope until it fell apart. At last he was free! He forgot all that Serena had said. He was hungry again.

Jumping the rail fence, William ran joyously down the road. He galloped all the way to the depot, hoping to get there on time. Just before he reached the station, the gray clouds turned to rain. William was drenched. Water dripped down from his horns, his tail, and his long beard.

The train was in the station. He went straight to the dining car, but nobody was there to greet him. There wasn't a soul on the station platform.

William was disappointed. Something was wrong! William cried "Maa-a-a" as loud as he could. He stamped his feet. He butted his horns against the side of the dining car. But nothing happened.

Finally he climbed the car steps. The doors were open, and he walked into the kitchen. His

old friend was not there. Instead, a new cook was working in the kitchen.

The new cook frowned. He did not like to see a wet bedraggled animal in his spotlessly clean kitchen.

"Get out!" he shouted, raising a frying pan. "You smell like a goat."

William's feelings were hurt. He fled to the car behind. Just then the train began to move out of Basalt station.

There was William in the day coach. The poor

goat gazed about in dismay. He saw plush seats and lamps that hung from the ceiling. He saw strange faces everywhere. The passengers were not very friendly. One lady shrieked, "Land's sakes, where did that dirty goat come from?" She jumped up onto a seat.

Another one pointed. "Look at that rope dangling from his neck! He must have broken out of the baggage car."

William stood perfectly still. He did not know what else to do. Then he gave a bleat of joy. Coming down the aisle was a familiar face. He leaped forward and nuzzled his horns against the blue uniform and brass buttons of the old conductor.

The conductor laughed loudly. "What's wrong, William?" he asked, stroking the little goat's wet head. "Didn't our new cook give you any dinner?"

"Maa-a-a," the goat replied sadly.

"We'll fix that right away. You just wait here!" The old conductor turned to face the passengers. "My friends," he said, "this is William, the dining-car goat. Every day he meets our train at Basalt station and the cook on the train gives him table scraps to eat. But there's a new cook on today and I guess he doesn't know our custom of feeding William."

Then the conductor disappeared into the dining car. A moment later he came back with the cook and a pan of food. He set the pan on the floor. William promptly emptied it.

"What are you going to do with the goat?" asked the cook.

"Put him off at the next stop," said the conductor. "That is Glenwood Springs."

"But Glenwood Springs is an hour's ride from Basalt. How can he ever get home again?"

The conductor smiled. "Oh, he'll get home all right. I will ask the station agent there to keep him overnight and send him back to Basalt on the morning train."

So William spent a night in the baggage room at Glenwood Springs. It was his first night away from home and he was most unhappy. He wondered if he would ever see the ranch house again, or Serena Beck, or the small red wagon, or his old friend the cook on the four o'clock train.

The thought of the friendly cook and his box of food reminded William that the hours were

passing and he was getting hungry once more. The station agent had forgotten to give him any food. William stamped his feet. "Maa-a-a," he cried again and again. He butted his horns against the door of the baggage room. No one came.

Suddenly he smelled apples, good, sweet, juicy apples like those in the orchard on the ranch at Roaring Fork Valley. He sniffed around. Beneath a pile of suitcases and packages he discovered a crate of apples.

William pushed aside the suitcases and packages with his horns. Then he jumped up and down on the crate until he broke its lid. After that he ate his fill of apples and went to sleep.

Next morning when the station agent opened the door of the baggage room, he was distressed to see the damage that William had done. He hastily shut the door and went to hunt for a dog collar and a chain. When he returned, he fastened the collar around William's neck and led him out to the platform. William went along quietly.

The morning train for Basalt puffed into Glenwood Springs and stopped. The station agent laid a wide plank from the platform up to the open door of the baggage car. Here William balked. He refused to board the train. The agent pulled on the chain while the baggage man got behind and pushed the little goat. William would not budge.

Then two brakemen in blue uniforms from the train crew came over to help the station agent and the baggage man. The dining-car goat stood stock still. One of the men whacked him with a brake club. Two others tried to pull him into the car by his horns.

"Maa-a-a! Maa-a-a!" cried William. Nobody had ever treated him like this before.

All of a sudden someone came to his rescue.
She was a girl with fiery blue eyes and flying red
pigtails. She rushed across the station platform
toward the man with the brake club. She pum-

meled him with her two fists and screamed, "You let my goat alone!"

There were tears of anger in her eyes. In that instant two more things happened. A woman hurried across the station platform, calling out, "Serena Beck, what *is* the matter?" And William broke away from the four men who were trying to force him into the baggage car. He nuzzled his horns gently into the girl's back. He was delighted to see Serena.

Everybody began talking at once.

"Quiet, please!" Aunt Clara said, "I want to hear what happened."

"Madame," said the station agent, "this goat wandered into a railroad train at Basalt yesterday afternoon and the conductor put him off here. He is a dining-car goat. He meets the same train every day and the cook feeds him table scraps."

"Yes, I know. He belongs to my niece here."

"Well," said the station agent, "we kept him here overnight and now we're sending him home to Basalt."

"My niece is going back on this train. Maybe she will take charge of her pet."

Serena patted the animal's back. "I am sorry

if I lost my temper," she said, "but I didn't want anyone to hurt William."

"We weren't hurting him, miss," said the man with a brake club. "We were only trying to put him in the baggage car."

"I will put him in," said Serena. "Come on, William!"

William followed her quietly up the plank into the baggage car.

Just then the conductor sang out, "Aa-all abo-oard!"

Aunt Clara called, "Can you manage that goat?"

"Yes, indeed," said the girl. "Daddy will be waiting at the station for me. Good-by, Aunt Clara! Thank you for a very nice visit."

"Good-by, dear!"

"Maa-a-a!" said William.

The engine whistle gave two long wails. The trainmen got on board the cars. When the wheels began to turn, Serena and William were standing side by side in the baggage car. They were going back to Basalt in the Roaring Fork Valley, back to daddy and mamma and the ranch house and the small red wagon. They were both very happy.

# Two Dogs on One Ticket

It was so hot you could have fried a hamburger
on the cinders in the railroad yards of a town on
the Illinois prairie. Two switchmen were leaning
against a freight car, trying to find shade from
the scorching July sun.

Suddenly one of them laughed and pointed
down the tracks. "Do you see what I see?" he
asked.

The other man shaded his eyes with his hand. "Sure," he nodded. "Grasshoppers."

Along the endless tracks came a green cloud. As the men watched, it became thousands of tiny things, flying, sweeping toward the yards.

"I see more than grasshoppers," the first man said. "Look!"

Both gazed intently, then roared with laughter. In the middle of the green army shuffled a big brown and white dog. His fur was matted, and long shaggy hair hid his eyes. He looked vaguely like an English sheep dog. His bushy tail waved aloft as he trotted along.

"Woof, woof!" he barked, as he snapped at the grasshoppers. He plodded past the switchmen and headed for the express office.

He pushed open the door with his nose. Expressman Strate looked up and he, too, laughed when he saw the intruder.

"Hello there, big fellow!" he said kindly, reaching for the animal's neck to see if he wore a collar. But there was nothing to tell the dog's name or his owner. A few grasshoppers fell off the matted coat, as the tail waved hopefully.

"Why, you're only a puppy," Mr. Strate con-

tinued. "You're not handsome and you certainly
need a bath, but I like your looks. How about a
drink first and something to eat?"

Two sharp barks answered this question. Mr.
Strate picked off the remaining grasshoppers and
set down a pan of water in front of his visitor. The
dog lapped thirstily. When he finished, he looked
up as if to say thanks, his tail beating on the floor
like a drum.

"I haven't much food," Mr. Strate said apolo-
getically, "but here's part of my lunch."

He opened the bottom drawer of his desk and
took out his dinner pail. The dog was alert in-
stantly. Mr. Strate offered a ham sandwich and
it disappeared in a single mouthful. The animal
sniffed for crumbs and whimpered a little. Then
he stretched himself on the floor beside a big
packing box and promptly went to sleep.

Mr. Strate studied him. The shipment in the
packing box was dry goods intended for a store in
Tobyhanna, Pennsylvania, and the address was
painted in black letters on the box. The dog was
sprawled in such a way that only the letters
"T-O-B-Y" could be seen. Mr. Strate said the
name aloud, "Toby."

The dog lifted his big shaggy head and looked at him.

"Is that your name, fellow?" Mr. Strate asked. "Well, okay, Toby it shall be."

The day droned on, the heat beating down on the express office. The dog slept on, worn out by his travels. In the afternoon Mr. Strate had two visitors, red-haired Rusty Bascomb and Hank Miller. Rusty and Hank loved the railroad yard and they usually stopped by on their way home from school. Occasionally Mr. Strate had odd jobs for them.

"Hello, boys," Mr. Strate greeted them, "I want you to meet Toby." At the mention of his name Toby rolled over lazily, and the two boys grinned. Hank ruffled the dog's fur, and Toby went back to sleep, while the boys went off to help Mr. Strate.

From then on Toby's home was the express room. At noon every day, when the whistle blew, Mr. Strate put a dish of food and a pan of fresh water by his desk. Toby gratefully accepted the offering. Things went on this way for several weeks.

One day toward the end of the summer Mr. Strate took his vacation. Before he left, he arranged for Rusty and Hank to come every afternoon to give Toby his food. And every day the boys prepared Toby's meal and gave him a pan of water.

The switchmen in the yard knew that Mr. Strate was away, and they too were concerned about Toby. At lunchtime, as they sat eating from their dinner pails, they tossed scraps of food to the dog. Toby gobbled everything that willing hands would give him. He would sit patiently in front of the men, his long hair dangling over his eager nose, and beg for food. He missed Mr. Strate, but by the end of the first week of the vacation, Toby was faring very well indeed.

Then on Sunday night something happened.

A big crate was eased carefully out of the baggage car and the expressman signed a receipt for "one crated dog." Rusty Bascomb, who was on hand, helped to trundle the crate onto a truck and into the station office.

It was a roomy crate and strongly built, with a side door and a wire-netting window. On it was

a card which said that the big red dog inside was being shipped from an Iowa kennel a hundred miles north to a new owner in St. Louis. Actually the dog was a pedigreed Irish setter named Rex, insured for more money than either Rusty or Hank had ever seen. Rex was to stay in the express office for about two hours, and then his crate would be put on another train for the journey to St. Louis.

In Mr. Strate's dimly lighted office the boys looked in at Rex. They thought he was unhappy. The longer they peered through the wire netting,

the more they were convinced they should do something for the setter.

"Poor pup!" Hank said sympathetically. "He must be cramped in that box."

"Yeah," Rusty agreed. "He's still got a long way to go. What do you say we let him out a couple of minutes to stretch his legs? It can't do any harm."

The boys cautiously unfastened the crate and with an eager yelp Rex bounded out. First he licked Rusty's hand in gratitude, then with a leap he was out the open door. Hank attempted a fly-

ing tackle but missed. As he rolled on the floor, the Irish setter vanished into the freedom of the night. Toby dashed after him, and the boys were a close second. The chase was on!

Both dogs were barking wildly. It was a mad race over the maze of storage tracks on which many cars stood waiting to be loaded or unloaded. Dogs and boys dodged in between the cars looming like shadows in the moonlight, to try and head off Rex.

"Good dog! Nice dog! Come here, pup!" they shouted.

It was all in vain. Rex had been cooped up too long to be lured back by kind words. Up and down the yards he ran, the boys in full cry. Toby enjoyed it thoroughly, but he was not much help. First he would chase Rex, then he would wheel back to see if the boys were all right. Rusty stumbled over a switch in the dark and sprawled full length, his face in the cinders, but was only scratched.

"We'll never catch him," he wailed. "Let's separate and try to corner him."

But Rex knew more than the boys did about

hunting, and he eluded them every time. Two or three switchmen joined in, while other yardmen watched the hue and cry. Hank ran full tilt into the end of a boxcar, which knocked the breath out of him, but he grunted and kept on going.

Finally the town clock tolled ten. The boys groaned. They were at the far end of the yard. To get back in time to help load the shipments on the 10:27 train for St. Louis, and unload the baggage as well, would take some running. Rex had vanished.

"Rusty!" Hank yelled, cupping his hands to his mouth. "We've got to go back."

They ran back to the office. They were breathless and they were frightened. The St. Louis train was due in five minutes and the box labeled "one crated dog" was empty.

Toby followed them hopefully. Once inside, as if he understood the situation, the dog lay down in front of the crate and partly backed into it. He thumped his tail as if to ask, "How can I help?"

The boys looked at each other. The same thought occurred to them both. Then Rusty said, "You're a smart dog, Toby."

Toby's tail beat a muffled tattoo inside the crate. Hank smiled.

"The waybill says 'one crated dog,' " Rusty said. "It doesn't say what kind of dog. And no one could have a better dog than good old Toby."

Hank was doubtful for a minute. Then he said, "We'll keep on looking for the setter. Then if the St. Louis man isn't satisfied with Toby, we can send him the setter. He will just think the two crates got mixed up."

"Sure, and in the meantime Toby will have a swell adventure. Here goes!"

The boys pushed Toby into the crate and made it fast. Then they thought they had better give him a pan of water. The train for St. Louis whistled in the distance. When it ground to a stop, the crate was on the depot truck along with boxes, packages, and suitcases for St. Louis. Toby looked through the wire netting, a bewildered expression on his shaggy face. How could his pals do this to him?

Hank and Rusty hung their heads.

The baggageman studied the waybill. One by one he checked off the items as they were loaded into his car. The boys held the crate till the last. They kept watching the yards, hoping vainly that Rex would return. Finally the crate was reached.

"One crated dog," the baggageman read. "Looks pretty heavy. I'll give you a hand. All right, boys, up she goes!"

A muffled yip from inside the car was Toby's farewell to his home. Rusty had a funny feeling in his stomach.

"Look, mister," he said hastily, "I think there's some mistake about that dog. Maybe he'd better stay here till it's fixed up."

The man adjusted his glasses. "No mistake, sonny. It says right here on the waybill, 'one crated dog.'"

"But I mean," Rusty began. Then he thought better of it. "I mean, we forgot to feed him today."

"Nonsense," said the man briskly. "It won't hurt a dog to skip a meal once in a while."

"All a-booooard!" bellowed the conductor, annoyed at the delay.

The baggage-car door was slammed shut, the whistle blasted, and the train roared off into the night. Hank and Rusty watched until it became

a small speck and disappeared. Then they walked slowly back to the office and closed the place for the night.

"Gee, I hope it's going to be all right," Rusty said.

"So do I," Hank agreed gloomily.

The following day, when they got to the office, someone was waiting patiently for them. It was Rex.

"Well, look who's here!" Hank cried.

"Get down!" Rusty said, as the dog leaped joyfully up on him, licking at his face. "Stop kissing me! Why couldn't you have come back last night? Now what are we going to do with you?"

Rex was frisky and he played rough. He kept jumping up and down, his tail going like a trip hammer. He pawed the boys and licked them.

"We needed you last night," Rusty said impatiently, "not today. Where were you?"

The setter hung his head as if he knew he was being scolded.

"That's better," Rusty said. "Now what are we going to do?"

Hank thought a moment. "We'll wait to see what happens. And we'll have to keep the setter."

So they led the unresisting Rex into the furnace room, fed him, and left a pan of water beside him. Then they locked the door.

The boys breathed easier when that was done. "My, I'm glad he came back," Hank said. "I didn't think he ever would. It's good he did."

Then Rusty laughed. "Wonder how old Toby is getting on in St. Louis. Gee, suppose the man knew what Rex looks like?"

"Never mind about that," Hank said. "We'll hear about it soon enough if he did. Anyway, we're taking good care of his dog all the time."

Within a short time the post office carried a special-delivery letter from St. Louis to the kennel in Iowa. It was as hot as the weather. It read:

*Dear Sir:*

*You are a swindler and a cheat. I paid you $100 for a pedigreed Irish setter, but you sent me a mongrel sheep dog. Maybe you think I do not know the difference. Well, I do. I am returning your beast by express collect in the crate in which he came. I want my money back at once.*

The afternoon the letter was written, Toby started off again on his travels. Back to the Illinois town he rode in the same crate with the same tag still on it. Hank and Rusty could hardly believe their eyes. They grinned broadly at each other as they unloaded the crate and they put it on the truck. They wheeled it to the express room. Toby's gleeful bark was a welcome sound.

"I guess that guy in St. Louis changed his mind about wanting a dog," Hank laughed.

"Yeah," Rusty agreed, "and boy, am I glad

Toby will be here when Mr. Strate gets back. He might be real mad if he found him gone."

The boys opened the crate and Toby shot out of it. He was a whirl of matted fur in his excitement, and he bounced up and down the room.

"Quiet, fella, quiet!" Hank said. "You're home now. It's all right."

Then the boys went after Rex. With a firm hold on his collar they led him to the crate, and got him safely inside. As they fastened the door, they sighed with relief.

"Sorry, pup," Hank said, "this time you stay in there till you get where you're going."

So Rex was loaded on the train for Iowa, and

before very long an equally angry letter went from there to St. Louis. It read:

*Dear Sir:*

*Your letter received. It does not make sense. I am at a loss to understand why you ordered a pedigreed Irish setter but returned him with an insulting message.*

*Rex is a healthy, thoroughbred, male puppy about seven months old. He is well trained. I sent you a pedigree guaranteed by the American Kennel Club. I resent your reference to a mongrel sheep dog and will not refund your money until you apologize.*

The customer in St. Louis insisted the dog was not an Irish setter and demanded his money back. The dog breeder held out for an apology. Letters flew back and forth.

In the meantime Mr. Strate returned. He was greeted enthusiastically by Toby.

That afternoon the boys stopped by as usual. "How did things go while I was away?" Mr. Strate asked when he saw them.

"Fine," Rusty said promptly. Then he hesitated. "I think you'll find everything in order, sir," he added.

"I hope so," Mr. Strate said. He looked at Rusty shrewdly. "The head office called me this morning about a complaint from a man in Iowa. Seems there was a mix-up over a dog. Do you know anything about it?"

"A mix-up over a dog, Mr. Strate?" Rusty repeated, to gain time.

"Yes. Over a mongrel sheep dog," and Mr. Strate looked pointedly at Toby, now snoozing in his favorite corner.

The boys exchanged glances.

"I guess we'd better tell you," Hank said at last.

"It might be a good idea," agreed Mr. Strate.

The boys told the whole story, one adding details the other forgot. Mr. Strate looked very stern. "Boys," he said, "I think this is going to work out all right, but fooling around with an express shipment is serious business, no matter how good a reason you have. I'd better make a few phone calls and see if we can straighten this out."

He reached for the telephone. He made two

long-distance calls. First he spoke to the man in St. Louis, and then to the dog breeder in Iowa. He told each one exactly what had happened. The boys listened intently and were relieved when they heard chuckles coming through the receiver.

The following day a familiar dog crate was taken off the baggage car at the Illinois station. Mr. Strate himself supervised its handling. But he allowed the boys to bring a pan of water for their old friend Rex.

Toby was on hand, bounding about and barking. Mr. Strate patted his shaggy head. "Rex will be at a good home in St. Louis tomorrow," he said, "and I'm mighty glad you're right here, Toby."

# Horse Sense

Peter Brent whistled a gay tune as he sat on the floor of the baggage car beside his two palomino horses, Grant and Julia. The train was rolling across the hot, dry, Texas prairie.

Peter was very happy. He had just turned sixteen and he was riding to the end of the track to get himself a job. Both his grandfathers had been trainmen. Ever since they had first told him stories of the tracks going west, he had wanted nothing in the world so much as to work for the railroad.

Peter had steam and steel in his blood. He loved the shining rails that marched to the sky-line and vanished in a pin point. He loved the engines and cars, the whistles and bells, and the sparks that shot up from the locomotives at night.

When he heard that the Texas Central was building a new line through the wilderness as far west as the Pecos River he knew his big chance had come.

His mother packed his clothes in a suitcase and gave him a bag filled with sandwiches, cookies, apples, and a whole roasted chicken. "Take care of yourself, Peter," she said. "I know you will be a good railroad man."

His father said, "Pete, I know how you feel about Grant and Julia. You have practically raised them yourself from the day they were foaled. Take them, son! The railroad company needs horses. They will pay you better money if you hire out with a good team."

So the palominos, named for the great Civil War general and his wife, had come with him.

Pop was right. In the Texas Central field headquarters at the end of the track Peter got a job as teamster with a surveying outfit.

He hitched the palominos up to a chuck wagon. Then he helped to load the wagon with food and supplies and fill its huge water cask. Pretty soon he climbed into the driver's seat, cracked his whip, and set out on a long trek.

Six surveyors on horseback rode with him. Their job was to drive wooden stakes into the hard earth to mark the line along which the new

railroad would be built. After them other men would come. These other men would lay ties and steel rails. They would set up telegraph poles and build stations for the trains that would follow. But five days after the surveyors set out, an accident happened, and for a while they stopped thinking about trains.

It was a hot day. Pete was driving the team along through the sage. Suddenly Julia tripped. She had stepped into a gopher hole hidden in the grass. She tried vainly to regain her balance, and Grant dragged frantically in the harness, but it was no use. The wagon toppled over.

Before it could be righted, the water cask had spilled its precious contents over the dry earth. Hardly a drop was left! Pretty soon every canteen in the party would also be empty. There would be no water at all.

Bull Stevens, the barrel-chested chief engineer in charge of the outfit, was very angry. "I should have known better than take on a kid with a team of farm horses," he growled.

"Julia couldn't help it," Pete said. "She stepped in a gopher hole."

"I know, I know," Bull Stevens said. "Just the same, we're in trouble. There hasn't been any rain in these parts for months."

The rest of the men were silent.

The plain was hot and dry and hard, baked like a johnnycake. Dust covered everything in sight—white, powdery, alkali dust. The weather-beaten railroad men on tired horses jogged along beside the wagon. A steady warm breeze from the south peppered their faces with grit.

Pete worried about Grant and Julia, too. The palominos were his pets. It grieved him to see them stumbling now from exhaustion.

Mr. Stevens studied the map he held on the saddle of his bronco. "This map shows a pond near here," he told Pete, "but I'm a horned lizard if I can tell where it is."

"Maybe the pond is dried up," Pete said.

"If it is, there's no water nearer than the Pecos River and that's thirty miles away," Mr. Stevens answered.

As he spoke, they entered a small grove of cottonwood trees. The withered leaves cast tiny patches of shade. Just at that moment Julia lunged forward in her traces and fell to the ground. The boy sprang from his seat with a sharp cry.

"Julia, Julia!" he cried. "What's the matter, old girl?"

Patting the mare, he coaxed her to stand up. But she only trembled and rolled her eyes.

Bull snapped a decision. "We'll camp here!" He nodded to Pete. "You stay with the team while the rest of us look for that pond. We had better find it," he added grimly.

"Yes, Mr. Stevens."

Pete unhitched his team and tied Grant to a tree. Julia was too weak to stand up. The boy wondered in alarm if she were dying. He brushed away a tear and sat down beside her. This was a fine way to start a railroad career, he thought. What if they never finished the job? He was fanning off the green flies when the hot weather became too much for him and he fell asleep.

The men searched in vain for the pond. Finally at sundown, one by one, they drifted back to camp. Each man slumped in his saddle. The horses' heads were hanging, too. Their manes drooped over their eyes.

Men and beasts munched on dry food. There was no water or coffee to wash it down. The horses pawed the dusty ground and neighed. It was their way of asking for a drink.

While the men were resting around the camp fire, Bull Stevens said, "We'll never locate a railroad line this way. I reckon the pond is gone. There is only one thing for us to do now. Head for the Pecos River. There's a chance we can make it by riding all night."

Dead silence fell. Not one of the men or horses was fit to journey so far that night.

Pete spoke first. "If you don't mind, Mr. Stevens, I'd like to stay here with Grant and Julia."

Bull glanced at Pete. "But I do mind," he said. "We'll leave the mare here with the wagon. We must travel light. You ride Grant! It's our only chance!"

"But Julia—" pleaded the boy. "The coyotes and buzzards will come here—"

"I'm sorry, Pete, but we must shoot her before we go."

"No, no. Something will happen—"

"Not likely. You don't want to leave her to suffer, do you?"

"No, of course not. But there's still a chance. Give Julia a little more time to rest. Then she'll get up. I know she will."

But the other surveyors were grumbling. The sooner they started, the better chance they had.

"We can't wait," Bull decided. "Our lives are at stake. If we ride all night while it's a bit cool, we may reach the river."

Pete stared at the dying camp fire. His heart pounded in his chest. The warm wind still blowing from the south curled the smoke around his face.

"Okay, I'll go," he said. "It's better to save one horse than lose two. But nobody will shoot Julia. I'll find water and come back to her."

"It's your horse. I'd shoot her if she were mine," Bull said, as he started off.

Pete tried again to rouse the mare. She was breathing hard and would not stir. Green flies buzzed around her. "You stay here, old girl. Wait for me; I'll come back!"

He stamped out the fire. Then he saddled

Grant and slowly mounted. The surveyors were carrying pistols, cartridge belts, empty canteens, and rations.

Julia neighed as they trotted away. Pete looked behind in the gathering dusk. He saw the mare struggle to her feet and totter after them a few steps. Then she fell down again and lay still. Her big head was turned toward them in mute appeal.

Pete choked a sob. "I'm going back!"

"Don't be a fool," said the chief, seizing his bridle. "You're coming with us!"

The railroad party rode in silence. Their throats were too swollen for speech. All of them knew that many painful miles lay between them and the lifesaving Pecos River. Horses and riders already were far spent.

Night's coolness brought some relief. Pete kept thinking of Julia. He felt like a traitor for leaving her alone. Yet he told himself that she had no chance to live unless he could find water for her.

Then, with little warning, the wind shifted. The weary men seemed not to notice, but Grant moved his big head restlessly. "He misses Julia," thought Pete, "and even now he'd turn back if I let him."

Now and then the chief struck a match to glance at his pocket compass. The moon rose. A cat's-claw tree in a clump of mesquite bushes cast weird shadows across the parched earth.

Suddenly in those shadows Pete heard the warning note of a diamond-backed rattler. Grant whinnied in fright. Rearing on his hind legs, while Pete clung tightly to the saddle, he pounded the glistening snake again and again with his hoofs.

"Good boy!" said Pete.

Grant sniffed the breeze with wide open nostrils. Is he just excited, Pete wondered, or does he smell something else? Grant made the decision and, with a quick turn, the palomino headed back toward camp. This time Pete let him have his way, and the chief made no protest.

Pete rode through the dark sage and buffalo grass, through stands of cottonwood and scrubby pine. He didn't need a compass—not with Grant picking the trail.

Moonglow on the deserted camp showed the chuck wagon still standing with an empty shaft where he had left it. The mare was gone! Pete wanted to believe that the coolness had revived her and she was able to walk again. But he was frightened.

Where could she be? Maybe coyotes had chased her off, or maybe she was looking for Grant and him.

Pete cupped his hands to his cracked lips and called hoarsely, "Juuu-lia! Juuu-lia!"

No thud of hoofs answered. There was no sound but the faint rustle of cottonwood trees. The boy patted Grant's neck and gave him a loose bridle.

"Go find Julia!" he said. "Oh, Grant, find Julia!"

Even on the hard, dry ground there were signs of Julia's struggle to her feet. Grant may have followed her trail, or he may have headed into

the breeze because he smelled water. Pete never
knew.

Grant moved steadily forward and after a
while they came to a glittering sheet of water
hidden in a pine grove. This, no doubt, was the
pond shown on Bull Stevens's map.

There was Julia!

The mare was standing in water up to her fet-
locks, nibbling at lush green grass that rimmed
the pond. She trotted toward Pete the instant he
shouted her name. Sliding out of his saddle, the
boy threw his arms around her neck.

"Julia, old girl," he said, "good old Julia! You knew your way to the pond, didn't you?"

Then he followed Grant into the pond for a long drink. Both boy and horse were trail-wise. They sipped slowly at first. The water was warm and a little muddy, but Pete would not have sold his share of it for a million dollars.

When they had finished drinking, Grant and Julia wanted to rest quietly by the pond. "I sure wish we could stay here," Pete said, "but we've still got a job to do. We've got to get water to the rest of the company."

He urged the horses back to camp. There he hitched them to the chuck wagon. Then he drove

to the pond and filled the water cask. A few minutes later he was driving westward toward the river.

The wagon rolled along with its priceless cargo. It bounced over the rough prairie land and jack rabbits ran to cover as it passed. Pete swayed in his seat, fighting sleep.

The apple-green sky was blazing red when he began to overtake the railroad surveyors. One man was sprawled on the ground beside his fallen horse. Pete revived them both with water.

From then on the boy picked up one man after another. He put a dipper of water to each man's dry lips and bathed his face. And he did not forget the horses.

Bull Stevens was the last. The barrel-chested chief engineer had left his tired bronco and was staggering in the direction of the Pecos River.

When Pete finally counted the score, all of the men and all of the horses were safe. It was not bad for a night's work. He smiled and turned to the chief engineer.

"And to think I wanted to shoot Julia!" Bull said. "She and Grant saved all of us."

Pete said, "They are good railroad horses, aren't they, Mr. Stevens?"

"No better anywhere. And you, Pete, have done all right on your first railroad job. It isn't an easy life, but it's a good one. Even after last night's experience, I still say that."

Pete suddenly laughed. Why, he had had an adventure that was just about as exciting as those his grandfathers had long ago. He really was a railroad man. After a long sleep he and Grant and Julia with the rest of the company would go on with the job of staking out the line of the new railroad across the hot, dry plains of Texas.

# The Bear
# in the Baggage Car

Eric, the polar bear, was riding on a train. It is
not an ordinary thing for polar bears to ride on
trains, but Eric was no ordinary bear.

Only a short time ago he had lived a wild, free
life in the frozen land of the Far North. Then
hunters had caught him and hauled him over

land and sea to the Central Park Zoo in New York City.

Now he was to have still another home. He was put in a small cage and loaded onto a baggage car bound for Utah.

Eric had enjoyed his big, roomy cage at the zoo but hated being in a small cage. His black eyes glittered with rage.

The baggage car in which he rode was coupled into a passenger train. It was just behind the engine and tender, where baggage cars are always placed. For two whole days Eric sulked in his cage. He listened to the rumbling of wheels and heard the engine whistle for grade crossings or stations. Eric listened to these sounds but he did not like them.

He remembered the still, cold, windless nights of the Far North where the stars blazed overhead with a fierce brightness. He remembered the nights when everything was quiet except the lapping of waves against an icy shore. Even when gales had howled across the dreary, snow-covered land, Eric had been happy. There, in the Northern wilderness, he had been a king.

He glared through the bars of his cage. Around him, outside the cage, other things were being shipped in the baggage car. Near him, so close that his claws could almost scratch it, stood a green upholstered davenport. Mysterious boxes, bundles, and packages met his eyes. Some of these were labeled "Candy" and others were labeled "Fruitcake." Eric could not read the labels, but he sniffed eagerly. The packages and boxes held something sweet. He knew that smell. He remembered the goodies children had fed him in the Central Park Zoo. If he could only get out of his cage he could sample these nice-smelling things.

He tested the cage with his big shoulders and strong white teeth and made a wonderful discovery! The bars were wooden! The whole cage was made of lumber!

Eric growled softly and set to work. Half an hour later he had smashed open his cage and stepped out. He looked around warily. This seemed too good to be true!

Pieces of the hated cage lay all over the floor. Eric had a lot more space for romping and exploring, but he was still a prisoner in the baggage car.

He looked at the windows. They were large enough for him to squeeze through, but the glass was protected by heavy iron bars. Eric did not like iron bars. With his heavy paws he broke the glass in three windows. It crashed down inside and outside the car.

He examined the door. There were doors on all four sides of the baggage car, but they were shut and locked. Eric grunted. Later he would decide whether he wanted to batter them down. Right now he would have some fun.

He wanted some of that candy and fruitcake. Like a greedy boy, Eric ripped open one box after another and stuffed his mouth with sweets.

Sometimes he would rise up to his full height of eight feet, standing on his hind feet, and pull boxes down from the top of the pile where they

had been neatly stacked. Usually he sat back on his haunches, and he seemed to chuckle to himself as he spilled chocolates all over the floor. In no time at all the baggage car was a sight!

Late that night the train stopped in Belle Plain. The station agent there came out to put some shipments aboard. He opened the side door of the dimly lighted car and gasped when he saw a huge wild animal munching fruitcake inside.

The agent yelled, slammed the door shut, and locked it. Then he shouted for help.

The conductor came running, but he had no weapon larger than a ticket punch. Other members of the train crew ran up. They all peeked in at Eric and then quickly slammed the door shut. Nobody knew what to do. None of them had ever met such a problem before. No one knew what to do with a polar bear, weighing nearly half a ton, who was loose inside a baggage car.

They thought and talked and argued. At last they decided to go on to the next town, which was called Boone. There they would have carpenters build a new cage and perhaps they could get Eric into it.

So they pulled into Boone, set the baggage car on a sidetrack, and the rest of the train went on. The town officials made a long-distance telephone call to a man who knew how to handle wild animals. This man kept a small zoo in Des Moines, the state capital.

"Come over right away!" they said. "An enormous polar bear has escaped from his cage. He's loose in the baggage car, and the baggage car is standing on a sidetrack in our town. He may break out of it. There is no telling what may happen! We are building a new cage and we want you to put him in it."

"I'll take the next train to Boone," said the zoo keeper. And he did.

Carpenters were building the cage from heavy timber and iron bolts. It was larger and much stronger than the old one.

For hours they worked. Hundreds of people, young and old, came to watch the excitement. They came in cars, on busses, in trucks, on foot, and in farm wagons. Policemen guarded the baggage car.

But Eric didn't try to escape. He was having too much fun.

At last the zoo keeper arrived and peeped into the car. There sat Eric.

"That bear must be very thirsty from eating so many sweets," said the zoo keeper. "If you want to keep him in good humor, you will have to give him ice. Lots and lots of ice. That will quench his thirst."

Several men offered to help. Soon they were shoving big and little chunks of ice through the broken car window. Eric loved ice. As fast as it was fed to him, he crunched it in his mighty jaws and growled for more.

Finally he grew tired of eating ice. And he was

tired of eating candy and fruitcake. He prowled
around the baggage car to see what other things
suited his fancy. The davenport was fun. He
bounced up and down on its springs. Eric was
enjoying himself a great deal when the davenport
gave way under the weight and smashed to the
floor.

The railroad men were very upset. They were
doing their best to save the valuable shipments.
The baggage car had a door at each end. While
Eric was rummaging around in the back of the
car, they would quickly slip in through the front

door, snatch a package or two, and rush out. When Eric was up in front, they would slip in at the back.

Finally the new cage was ready. A fine, roomy cage it was. The men set it on a baggage truck and backed the truck up to the baggage car. Inside of the cage were placed a large pan of water with chips of ice floating in it, and a chunk of raw meat.

Eric glanced around when he heard the door

click open. Hundreds of curious people waited in tense silence. But they need not have worried, for Eric just yawned. He was tired now and drowsy, and his stomach began to ache. He wanted a fresh drink of water and a nap. He walked slowly through the open door and into his new cage.

Late that night he was again speeding on a train to Utah.

In the zoo at Salt Lake City, Eric settled down happily. He forgot all about his troubles in the baggage car. He slept in the shade and swam in his private pool. Sometimes when the weather was very hot, his keepers let blocks of ice down into his bath and he liked that very much. And sometimes happy children tossed peanuts or crackerjack to him. Then he seemed to remember that once, for a few hours, he had enjoyed candy and fruitcake on a speeding train.

# The Beavers
# that Flooded the Track

One autumn night as Mr. Thayer, the boss of the
railroad track crew, was fishing in the woods
beside the tracks, he saw a curious sight. There
were six little noses sticking up out of the moon-
bright water, and each nose made a tiny ripple
as it moved upstream.

Mr. Thayer grinned. "I see that Brownie the beaver is taking his family for a swim," he said to himself. "Heigh-ho! It looks like trouble for the railroad!"

He sat very still and watched. He counted four beaver kittens trailing their father and mother. All six paddled along quietly. They swam with their hind feet, which were webbed like a duck's, and they used their broad flat tails to steer by.

Pretty soon he saw Brownie climb up on the bank near the culvert that carried the stream under the railroad track. Mr. Beaver shook the water off his thick brown fur and looked around. Everything was quiet. The young ones began to play water tag, while Mrs. Beaver perched herself on a flat rock and waited.

Mr. Thayer waited, too, hardly daring to breathe. It was fun to watch the wild creatures go about their business in the moonlight. Brownie walked over to a gleaming white willow tree that grew near the creek. Rearing on his hind legs, he braced himself with his scale-covered tail and held the trunk of a small tree with his front paws.

Mr. Thayer could hear the beaver's strong

teeth nibbling the trunk. They cut a notch through the bark and then another notch about three inches below it. After that they tore out a chunk of wood between the notches. In no time at all the ground was littered with white chips.

And then the tree fell. *Cr-r-ack! Smash!* All six beavers suddenly plopped into the water. They were not taking any chances. A fox or some other unfriendly animal might be lurking in the woods nearby and hear the noise. The safest place for a beaver in time of danger is under water.

Mr. Thayer listened. He heard only the night breeze rustling the trees. He smelled pine and wild honeysuckle. By and by Brownie's head poked cautiously above the water. Then the whole family scrambled out on dry land.

The four beaver kittens played beside the stream, ready to dive in a jiffy if anything went wrong. Mr. and Mrs. Beaver headed for the fallen tree.

First they stripped off the branches with their teeth. Then they laid the branches aside so they could use the bark for food and the peeled white sticks for their dam and their house.

Their next job was to cut up the trunk into short lengths. After that they pushed and rolled a log to the water's edge. This was hard work.

Mr. Thayer knew that Brownie and his wife were getting ready to make a dam. He knew that when it was finished there would be a pond at least three feet deep where the beavers would build themselves a home. He only hoped that the pond would not cover the railroad track. If it did, Mr. Thayer and his gang of men would have to break the dam to clear the track for passing trains.

The track boss had often seen these beaver

houses with their big, dry, single room above the water level and their passageways leading to the bottom of the pond. He knew that Brownie needed his house. He could go in and out of it without being seen by his enemies and in the cold winter he could reach his store of bark and water-plant roots for food even if the water froze nearer the surface.

But as much as Brownie and his family needed their home, they could not be allowed to flood the tracks.

Mr. Thayer was so busy thinking about the beavers that he forgot his fishing. Suddenly a

shiny fish got caught on his hook. It splashed around frantically. Brownie stopped pushing his log and slapped the water with his broad flat tail. *Ker-flop!* That noise was a warning for his family. "Hide as fast as you can!" it said.

All six beavers dove into the creek.

Mr. Thayer sighed. The beavers had found out that he was there. He felt sure that they would not go back to work until he was gone.

"Well, there's no use staying here any more," the track boss said to himself. "I won't be able to see them build a dam after all."

So he picked up his fishing pole and the fish he had caught and walked home through the shadowy woods.

The next morning Mr. Thayer fried his fish for breakfast. Then he began his day's work. He and his men chug-chugged over the railroad line in a motor speed car to see that the track was safe. But when they came to the creek, they could go no further. The rails were covered by a wide pond that glittered in the sunshine.

"A beaver dam!" said one of the men.

"Yes," said Mr. Thayer. "I saw them starting

to build it last night when I was out fishing."

The dam was made of logs, mud, stones, driftwood and water plants. It plugged up the culvert, forcing the water to flow over the track. It was built strongly.

"It's too bad they did all the work for nothing," said Mr. Thayer, "but we can't let them flood the railroad line. All right, boys, let's clear it away!"

The men put on their hip boots and attacked the dam with long iron pike poles. The job was not easy. Finally they finished. The pond sank into the creek, the creek flowed through the culvert beneath the track, and the line was clear again.

"Maybe that will discourage Brownie," said Mr. Thayer.

But Brownie and his family needed a deep pond in which to build a house for the winter. The only way for them to get such a pond was by making a dam. Brownie had picked the culvert as a good place for a dam, and so that very night he set to work again.

Mr. and Mrs. Beaver cut down more trees with

their sharp teeth. They cut up the trunks into short lengths. They rolled and floated the logs. They carried loads of stones and mud and water plants, hugging the stuff close to their chests as they walked on their hind legs.

By morning they had built another dam. They were very proud of it. Once more the railroad track was flooded by a pond that glittered in the sunshine. Once more the track gang came along in their speed car, tore down the dam, and drained off the pond.

"This is too much like work," said Mr. Thayer,

wiping the sweat from his face. "We must put a
stop to it!"

"But how?" asked one of his men. "There is a
law against killing beavers."

Mr. Thayer grinned. "I wouldn't hurt Brownie
or his family. I have always liked the busy little
fellow. You know, farmers use scarecrows in their
fields to keep the crows away. What we need is a
scare-beaver."

"And what kind of contraption is that?"

Mr. Thayer scratched his head. "I remember
how the beavers were scared by the noise of a
fish splashing in the water on my hook. Now, if
we could rig up an alarm clock or something to
make an awful racket, it might do the trick."

"But alarm clocks run down. Suppose the
beavers come back after the alarm stops?"

"We must fix up a noise that won't stop," said
Mr. Thayer, and he told the gang what to do.

They collected a lot of empty old tin cans and
put them in the creek near the culvert. They fastened these cans with wire in such a way that the
current would rattle and bang them together all
night long.

The boss chuckled. "When Brownie, the beaver, hears this racket, I'll bet he will move his family further on up stream."

But Mr. Thayer guessed wrong. The next morning, when the track gang rode the speed car, there, glittering in the sunshine, was a brand new pond. It flooded the rails at the same old place. A flock of wild ducks flew up from the pond, honking across the blue sky.

Mr. Thayer groaned. "All right, boys, let's go!"

Again they labored with their long iron poles until they cleared out the new dam from the culvert and drained the track of water.

While they were resting, the boss said, "Our tin cans didn't work! Now we have to think of something else."

One man said, "We could spread a chicken-wire fence across the culvert at each end to keep the beavers out."

Mr. Thayer shook his head. "That wouldn't do. They would only build their dam at one end of the culvert instead of inside it."

Another man asked, "Why couldn't we use some bad-smelling stuff like the kind that keeps off mosquitoes or the kind that protects trees and bushes from rabbits and other animals?"

"Maybe we could," said the boss. "It's worth trying, anyhow."

So the men piled on board the motor speed car and chug-chugged into town. They bought some strong-smelling stuff at the drug store. Then they rode back to the culvert and smeared it on all the trees nearby, a few inches above the roots.

"I hope that works," said Mr. Thayer.

But next morning, it was the same old story. A wide pond glittering in the sunshine covered the railroad track. Mr. and Mrs. Beaver were doing their best to get ready for the winter. Not even the strong-smelling stuff could stop them.

Mr. Thayer knew that if he let the pond stay

there, the beavers would build themselves a house
and would store a food supply at the bottom of
the pond. But no railroad train could run while
the track was flooded with a deep pond. So once
more the boss ordered his men to clear away the
dam.

After the job was done, he said to them, "Our
tin cans were not good and our bad-smelling stuff
was not good. Now I have a better idea. Beavers
like to work in the darkness. Maybe if we keep a
lantern burning all night it will drive them away."

So that night they hung a lighted lantern on
top of a pole and drove the pole into the creek bed
near the culvert. They knew it would swing back
and forth during the night. They hoped it would
keep the beavers from working.

But what do you think happened? The next

morning, when the track gang chug-chugged to the creek in their speed car, they found the rails covered by a new pond. And that wasn't all. The rising water had put out the light and broken the lantern.

Once more the men cleared out the culvert and drained off the pond so the trains could run again. Mr. Thayer was very much annoyed.

"The job of tearing down a new dam every day or two is a nuisance," he said. "Our beaver friends are much too busy. This time I have a real plan to make them move."

"But how?" asked one of his men.

"You will see," said the track boss.

Mr. Thayer wrote out a report to his own boss, the roadmaster. And the roadmaster took up the matter with other officials of the railroad company.

By and by the word came back to Mr. Thayer, "Go ahead with your plan!"

The track boss told his men what to do. That night they quietly set special traps for Brownie's family. And the next morning, when they chug-chugged over to the creek in their speed car, they

found Mr. and Mrs. Beaver and the four beaver kittens caught in the traps.

The beavers were crying like children, as beavers do when they are frightened, but not one of them was hurt.

"Now don't you worry!" Mr. Thayer said to the beavers. "We are going to take good care of you. We are going to make you very happy."

The track men put all six beavers into one big cage. Then they loaded the cage on their speed car and rode into town with it. There they found an airplane waiting. Mr. Thayer got on board the plane, lugging the cage with him.

Pretty soon the plane took off. It swooped through the blue sky like an eagle, over forests and lakes. Finally it landed at a lonely spot beside a winding creek. Mr. Thayer stepped out and set his cage on the ground.

"Now," he told the beavers, "you can build a dam and a house for the winter and nobody will disturb you. The railroad is a hundred miles away."

With that, he opened the cage door. All six

beavers tumbled out. They raced toward the creek, and before you could say "Jack Robinson" the whole family plopped into the clear shining water.

Mr. Thayer chuckled. Then he picked up the empty cage, climbed aboard the airplane, and went back to his job of bossing the track gang. The railroad line would not be flooded now, and Brownie and his family would soon have a snug house for winter.

# The Circus-train Elephant

The circus train was on its way to town. In her
private railroad car Suzy, the biggest elephant
in the circus, was dozing happily. Her car was
fitted out with all the things an elephant might
need, and her stall was piled with sweet-smelling
hay. Nearby, on a bunk overlooking the stall, Mr.
Scott, Suzy's trainer, was fast asleep.

Suzy liked Mr. Scott. Whenever she asked for anything he knew what she wanted. He understood her language. Sometimes at night the train rocked around a curve. The sudden jerk would make Suzy nervous. She would reach up her long trunk to the edge of Mr. Scott's bunk to find out if he were still there. A pat of his hand made her feel much better.

"You're all right, my girl," he would say. "Now go to sleep!"

Just tonight Mr. Scott had been very understanding. The train had been passing through fields of ripe watermelons. Suzy had smelled the large sweet melons immediately. There was nothing she liked quite as well as melons. She had wanted to tell Mr. Scott about it. So she raised her long trunk in the darkness. It had landed on the bell cord that signals the engineer to stop the train. In some way she pulled the cord.

The cars bumped together in a jerky stop. Trainmen got off with lanterns. They walked up and down to see what was wrong, flashing a light into each car, one at a time.

Pretty soon they opened the door of Suzy's

private car. The elephant was quietly eating hay.
Mr. Scott was still in his bunk. The train conductor looked around. He was puzzled.

"Did you pull that cord?" he asked.

Mr. Scott shook his head. "No, I didn't. But
I'll bet I know who did. I think my elephant
friend here may have done it by mistake."

The conductor looked at the bell cord and then
at Suzy.

"Well, why don't you watch her?" he asked in
annoyance. "She's stopped the train and everyone is racing around looking for the trouble."

He was still muttering when he left. The engine whistle tooted four times. Pretty soon the circus train was again roaring through the night.

Then Mr. Scott climbed down from his bunk. He went to a closet and came back with a big, red, juicy slice of watermelon.

"Is this what you want?" he asked. "I saved it especially for you."

Suzy's long trunk shot out. With three bites she ate the whole slice of melon, rind and all. Now she was swaying gently from side to side, as elephants do when they are happy.

Just before sunrise the circus train stopped on the edge of a town. It stopped on a sidetrack beside a large pasture lot.

The men lit their gas torches and began to unload the train by the flaring light. Pretty soon excited boys and girls swarmed around the lot from all over town to watch the fun.

Mr. Scott led Suzy out of her car. Then the other elephants lumbered down the gangplanks out of their cars. In no time at all the whole place

was alive with elephants, camels, zebras, and prancing milk-white horses.

Next the red and gold wagons and chariots were rolled down from flatcars. Then came a noisemaker on wheels, the gilded calliope, that always brought up the end of a circus parade.

Enormous rolls of canvas were tossed off the cars, then tons of rope, tent poles, and folded chairs. After that the men known as roustabouts started to raise the big tent. Suzy and the other

elephants helped to tighten the ropes that held it in place.

The elephants trumpeted. Lions and tigers roared. Dogs barked. Horses neighed. Boys began asking the elephant boss, "Please, sir, may I carry buckets of water for the elephants?"

Mr. Scott put them to work. The boys took turns at working the pump. They worked long and hard. Sweat rolled down their faces. As fast as each bucket was filled, willing hands carried it to a thirsty elephant.

While all this was going on, rosy dawn came.
Then a hot sun blazed in the sky. Just before the
boys got as far as Suzy with their water pails, the
pump ran dry. There was no water for Suzy. Mr.
Scott was busy some distance away and he did
not realize Suzy's plight.

The big elephant trumpeted in vain for a
drink. She stamped her feet. But the men were so
busy that nobody noticed her.

Suzy was tied to an oak tree near the railroad
track. She tugged at the rope. It was too strong

to break, no matter how much weight she threw against it.

But Suzy was smart. She knew that force was not always the best way to solve a problem. Patiently she worked on the knot with the finger at the end of her trunk. She could do a lot with that finger.

At last the knot was untied. Just as the loose end of the rope fell to the ground, Suzy heard a bugle call. It was the signal for the circus to line up for the big parade down the road and into Main Street.

Suzy knew that her place was at the head of the line. But right now the circus parade would have to wait. Suzy had other business to attend to. She was very thirsty.

The driver of the gilded calliope waited sleepily in his seat. The plumed horses waited. The clowns waited. The brass band waited. The ladies in pink tights with short fluffy skirts waited. They all waited while the big elephant looked for a drink.

Suzy went straight to the pump, kicking aside the empty buckets that stood in her path. She shook the pump handle with her trunk. There was not a drop of water!

Suzy snorted. She yanked off the pump handle and stamped on it. Then she trotted down the road to town.

Mr. Scott ran after her, with a small crowd of men and boys at his heels. Suzy headed into Main Street. The driver of a large moving van saw her

coming and tried to block her way. With a mighty shove, Suzy pushed over the truck and kept on going.

In no time at all the sidewalks were empty. People screamed. They rushed into the post office and stores and houses. They shut and locked the doors. There wasn't even a dog left on the street.

A man was watering his front lawn with a hose. When he saw the elephant, he stopped suddenly. He turned off the water and ran.

Suzy put the dripping end of the hose into her mouth. No more water came out. Twisting her trunk around the hose, she yanked it off the faucet. Then she used it like a whip to beat the side of the house.

Pretty soon she tired of this sport. Suddenly the wind changed and the big elephant smelled something good. Something she wanted very much. Tramping through a bed of petunias, she cut across the yard, broke down the fence, and entered a field. There on all sides lay dozens and dozens of big plump watermelons, ripe in the summer sun!

Trumpeting with glee, Suzy set to work. One after another, she squashed open the melons with a light tap of one foot. She was gorging herself on the red juicy fruit, rinds and all, when Mr. Scott caught up with her.

The men and boys who had followed the elephant trainer stood back at a safe distance. But Suzy had no desire to hurt anyone. Mr. Scott grinned as he watched her. He knew there was nothing he could do about it until the gentle beast had satisfied her taste for melons.

"This feast will cost the circus company a few

dollars," he said to the group standing around him, "but it's worth the price. It will advertise the show. Besides, Suzy really does like melons."

After a while Suzy stopped eating. Mr. Scott went up to her.

"Has my girl had enough?" he asked. "All right, let's go!"

Suzy wrapped her trunk around the trainer. Then she lifted him into the air and carried him all the way back to the circus lot.

"Here comes Suzy!" shouted the crowd, and the other circus elephants trumpeted a loud welcome. Everybody was glad.

The band struck up a lively air. Boys and girls cheered and shouted and clapped their hands. And the bright parade, half a mile long, swung down the road toward Main Street with Suzy marching proudly at the head.